little bee books

New York, NY
Text copyright © 2022 by Alice B. McGinty
Illustrations copyright © 2022 by Tomoko Suzuki
All rights reserved, including the right of reproduction
in whole or in part in any form.
Manufactured in China RRD 0522
First Edition
10 9 8 7 6 5 4 3 2
Library of Congress Cataloging-in-Publication Data is available upon request.
ISBN 978-1-4998-1217-6

For information about special discounts on bulk purchases,
please contact Little Bee Books at sales@littlebeebooks.com.

littlebeebooks.com

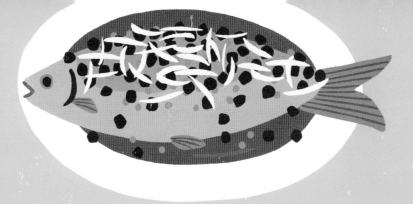

Feasts and Festivals Around the World

From Lunar New Year to Christmas

by Alice B. McGinty   **illustrated by** Tomoko Suzuki

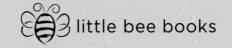
little bee books

Acknowledgments
Thank you to these wonderful people who provided the details that brought this book to life: Fei Du, Keke Li, and Jiayuan Liu from China; Paddy Lynch and Breda, PJ, and Louise Roche from Ireland; Kanittha Fay from Thailand; Rania Ahmed Youssef from Egypt; Helena Björk and Anna Keck from Sweden; Christopher Cheng from Australia; Afoma Okoli and Daniel Aneke Okoli from Nigeria; Bomi Kim and her family from Korea; Catherine Ann Velasco and Olga del Carmen Palma from Bolivia; Tina Forman and her mother Ida DeChellis from Italy; and Courtney and Christopher Price from Scotland.

Author's Note
Modern calendars follow the sun, but ancient calendars—and ancient holidays—follow the moon. These lunar holidays fall on different days each solar year, since the moon's orbit is shorter than a solar month. The Lunar New Year begins between January 21 and February 21, when the first new moon appears.

For Bomi
— **ABM**

For Chisato
— **TS**

Let's celebrate! It's time to feast.
The holidays are here!
There's food and fun around the world,
each season of the year!

Who celebrates the New Year?

China!

Begin the lunar year
with lanterns glowing red
Feast on fish and dumplings
for a lucky year ahead.

Lunar New Year

Spring Festival

In China, for the Lunar New Year, or Spring Festival, the youngest child decorates the family's door in red. Families gather on New Year's Eve for a "reunion dinner," feasting on lucky foods like fish (for prosperity) and homemade dumplings (for wealth). Who'll find the gold coin hidden in a dumpling? During the fifteen-day festival, families visit elders to wish them health, and children receive red envelopes with gift cards or money. The celebrations end with the Lantern Festival. Communities send lanterns into the air and eat sweet rice balls for good luck. Lunar New Year is one of the most celebrated events in the world. Many East Asian countries, like Korea and Vietnam, also celebrate this important holiday.

Now, cross the world to find a scene
where buds burst open into green!

Who celebrates in spring?

Ireland!

Saint Patrick's Day! A green parade.
Huge meals of Irish stew.
A shamrock painted on your face —
three leaves, bright and new!

March 17th

St. Patrick's Day

Saint Patrick's Day, or the Feast of Saint Patrick, falls on March 17th and celebrates the patron saint of Ireland. It's a religious holiday that also celebrates Irish culture. Kids collect shamrocks (three-leaved clovers), dress in green, and take part in their local parade by playing Irish music and singing. Families and friends celebrate with a huge meal, including lamb stew, bacon (like ham), cabbage, meat pies, colcannon (creamy mashed potatoes with cabbage), soda bread, rhubarb tart, and apple cake!

Head east to find a cooling treat . . .
a festival that beats the heat.

Who celebrates in April?

Thailand!

Cleanse yourself. It's Songkran!
The weather makes you sweat,
so feast on cooling dishes
and get very, very wet!

April 13th – 15th

Songkran

Thailand has three seasons—hot season, cold season, and rainy season. Each April, during the hottest part of the hot season, comes Songkran, the famous Buddhist water festival and Thai New Year. Families visit elders, pouring water over their hands and receiving blessings for the coming year. They clean house and enjoy a big meal, including cold dishes such as khao chae (kow SHEH) (rice soaked in floral water), mango and sticky rice, and spicy papaya salad. Then they gather for parades and celebrate the coming year by splashing water on each other to wash away any sadness. Some gently sprinkle each other with fragrant water and others soak one another with water guns!

A journey to the Middle East brings honored customs— and more feasts!

Who *sometimes* celebrates in spring?

Egypt!

Two important Muslim feasts, rotate into spring.
One with sweets, the other meats, both bring joyful things!

The End of Ramadan

Eid al-Fitr

Muslims worldwide observe two big lunar Eids (feast holidays) which rotate through the year. Eid ul-Fitr (EED uhl-FIH-ter), Festival of Breaking the Fast, falls in May of 2022. It celebrates the end of Ramadan, a lunar month when Muslims don't eat or drink during daytime hours. In Egypt, friends and relatives gather at dawn to break the fast with sweet dates. At lunch, they feast on foods such as lentil soup, stuffed grape leaves, and Ghoriaba, Egyptian butter cookies.

The larger Eid ul-Adha (EED uhl-AHD-ah) comes about two months later, when families buy a sheep to honor the prophet Abraham's sacrifice to God. They give a third of the meat to the poor, a third to relatives, and keep a third, which they barbeque and roast and serve over fatta (rice, toast, and tomato sauce). During both holidays, people say prayers, buy new clothes, give gifts, and go on outings.

Want longer days for summer fun?
Head north where Earth tilts towards the sun.

Who celebrates in June?

Sweden!

Raise the maypole. Dance and sing!
There are many games to play!
Friends all share a smorgasbord.
Midsummer's Eve—Hooray!

Between
June 19th and 26th

Mid-Summer

After winter's short, dark days, Sweden celebrates summer, where in some places the sun doesn't set at all! The day before summer's longest day is Midsummer's Eve. Families pick wildflowers and make wreaths to wear. Then they gather around the town's maypole, the accordion plays, and they dance and sing. They picnic, play games, and then follow musicians through the streets dancing the Small Frog Dance (Små grodorna) and more! Later, neighbors and friends share a huge smorgasbord (SMOR-gas-board) (buffet) including pickled herring, smoked salmon, shrimp, potato salad, and quiche! It's one of Sweden's biggest holidays!

Now hit the southern hemisphere.
It's summer in December here!

Who celebrates in summer?

Australia!

Surfers wearing Santa hats?
It's Christmas on the beach!
Prawns cooked on the barbeque—
there's plenty more for each!

December 25th

Christmas
in
Summer

South of the equator in Australia, it's summer when Christmas rolls around, so Aussies celebrate outdoors! Because it's HOT, they pack backyards and beaches wearing Santa hats, bringing coolers (eskies) of cold drinks and salads, and grilling prawns on the barbeque for a huge lunch. Some families make a traditional home meal of roast turkey. No matter where the meal is, it's likely to include Christmas crackers (pull the ends and they crack like a firecracker and out pops a prize) and a dessert of flaming Christmas pudding (perhaps with some sixpence coins hidden inside)!

Want another holiday?
Harvest season's underway!

Who else celebrates in summer?

Nigeria!

Harvest a yam, the king of the crops.
Celebrate with a parade!
Enjoy the New Yam Festival,
with drums and masquerade!

Early August

New Yam
Festival

In Nigeria, yams are not only the king of crops, but the first crop harvested. Big yams and a plentiful harvest are signs of a farmer's strength. During the New Yam Festival, the Igbo people thank God and their forefathers for giving them the strength to farm. Each community digs up their most enormous yam. After the chief or elder cuts it up, it's roasted and shared with the community. Kids love watching the yams roast and participating in the joyful masquerades and parades with drums, music, stomping, and dancing.

Where else do we harvest food?
Too many countries to include!

Who celebrates in autumn?

Republic of Korea!

Honor ancestors and elders
in this special harvest fest.
Small, half-moon shaped rice cakes
are what everyone loves best!

The day of
the harvest moon

Chuseok

On the eve of the harvest moon, the Republic of Korea celebrates the lunar holiday of Chuseok (CHEW-sok), the Korean Thanksgiving. Families return to their hometowns to visit parents. Many prepare a table of fruits, soups, and fish, and kneel before it to pay tribute to ancestors and give thanks for a plentiful harvest. They eat a huge meal, including jeon (meat and vegetable pancakes) and most important, songpyeon (SONG-pyon), colorful half-moon shaped rice cakes filled with chestnuts or sesame seeds and honey. The half-moon shape shows the potential to grow!

Hop the ocean—the equator, too,
to find this feast that's *not* for you!

Who celebrates in November?

Bolivia!

Remember those who've passed
with a feast of cakes and bread.
Their souls come back to visit,
on the Day of the Dead.

November 1st-2nd

The Day of The Dead

At the beginning of South America's summer, from noon on November 1 (The Day of the Dead) until noon on November 2nd (All Saints Day), Bolivians believe that the souls of the dead come to visit. Families prepare a "mesa" (table) as an altar for relatives who've died. They bake pastries, prepare foods and drinks the relative loved, and make breads with clay faces resembling theirs. The feast gives souls energy for the journey from the afterworld. Ladder-shaped bread helps them climb back to heaven and a candle lights their way. Families visit the cemetery, where they've decorated tombstones, to pray and share memories and food. This holiday originated in Mexico and is now celebrated in many countries.

Now it's time to journey north.
A different harvest gathers forth.

Who else celebrates in autumn?

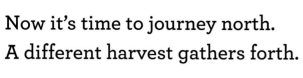

The U.S.A!

Turkey, stuffing, pumpkin pie . . .
it's Thanksgiving Day!
Families come together
from close and far away!

4th Thursday
in November

Thanksgiving
Day

For centuries, Indigenous Peoples, such as the Wampanoag tribe, have held harvest celebrations. In October of 1621, some members of the Wampanoag tribe feasted with European pilgrims, and out of this event, the Thanksgiving holiday began. Now, many families in the United States of America get together to give thanks for happy things—including each other. A traditional Thanksgiving meal includes turkey, stuffing, potatoes, cranberry sauce, and pumpkin and apple pies. Many families also include foods from their own ethnic backgrounds.

Move into winter and cross the big sea,
to discover another feast filled with glee.

Who celebrates in winter?

Italy!

Is it seafood that you smell?
Catch a whiff of all those dishes!
Italians *fast* on Christmas Eve . . .
with the Feast of Seven Fishes!

Christmas Eve

The Feast of
Seven Fishes

This holiday began as a fast, not a feast! Roman Catholics have a rule not to eat meat on Christmas Eve because Christmas is a feast day. People followed the rule and ate seafood on Christmas Eve—but they ate a LOT of seafood, and Christmas Eve became a time to feast on fishes. In Southern Italy, this holiday is called La Vigilia. Now, most people go to the market for fresh fish and enjoy a huge meal, often with MORE than seven fishes—baccalà (salted cod), mussels, clams, crabs, octopus, sole, scallops, shrimp, and the biggest delicacy—an oily eel, cut into steaks and fried!

This joyous year is almost done.
What's up next for feasts and fun?

Who else celebrates in winter?

Scotland!

Hogmanay on New Year's Eve—
the world's brightest party!
Light a torch and join the crowd!
Everyone eats hearty!

New Year's Eve

Hogmanay

In Scotland, the last day of the year is called Hogmanay—New Year's Eve. Scotland's capital, Edinburgh, hosts a huge street party with carnival rides and vendors selling stovies (sliced potatoes cooked in fat), fish and chips, waffles, crepes, and more. That evening, pipes sound and drums beat as thousands of people light torches and parade through the city toward Edinburgh Castle for music and Scottish dancing. At midnight, a cannon sounds and a bright fireworks display welcomes the new year. Everyone sings "Auld Lang Syne" (written by Scottish poet Robert Burns).

A year of celebrations!
It's the end—but don't lose heart.
Another festive, feastful year
is just about to start!

The U.S.A

Scotland

Ireland

Sweden

Italy

Nigeria

Bolivia

Feasts and Festivals Around the World

Egypt

Republic of Korea

China

Thailand

Australia